Stéphanie Bélanger

Illustrated by Chantelle Davie

Little Girl and Young Woman

ISBN: 978-1-4866-2313-6
eBook ISBN: 978-1-4866-2314-3

Word Alive Press
119 De Baets Street Winnipeg, MB R2J 3R9
www.wordalivepress.ca

WORD ALIVE
—P R E S S—

Cataloguing in Publication information can be obtained from Library and Archives Canada.

To Little Stéphanie,
welcome home to my heart.

"Little Girl," said Young Woman, "why are you crying?"

"Because," said Little Girl, "my friend said she doesn't want to play with me anymore."

"Come here." Young Woman opened her arms so Little Girl could crawl into her lap.
Young Woman gently stroked Little Girl's hair.

"My heart hurts," said Little Girl, crying.

"Yes," said Young Woman. "You have a broken heart. A broken heart heals, but it takes time."

They sat quietly for a while.

Suddenly, Little Girl turned and saw a tear trickle down Young Woman's face.

"Young Woman," said Little Girl somewhat perplexed. "Why are you crying?"

"Because," said Young Woman, "the one I love loves another."

Little Girl reached her hand up and placed it gently on Young Woman's face. "Does your heart hurt?" she asked very gently.

"Yes," whispered Young Woman.

Little Girl turned to face Young Woman and placed her forehead on Young Woman's forehead. She placed her other hand softly on Young Woman's other cheek.

"Then we both have broken hearts," Little Girl said quietly.

They sat like that for a while.

Little Girl spoke first. "How long does a broken heart take to heal?"

"As long as it needs," Young Woman answered.

"When will we know our hearts have healed?"

"Oh, we'll know, Dear One," Young Woman answered gently. "We'll know."

"Can I stay with you until that happens?" asked Little Girl a third time.

"Oh yes, Little One. You can stay with me until long after our broken hearts have mended."

Little Girl looked up at Young Woman. "It will be nice to heal my heart with yours."

"My heart won't heal unless you are with me," replied Young Woman tenderly. "You are me and I am you. I need you and you need me."

Again, they sat quietly.

Suddenly they both stood and walked along, Young Woman carrying Little Girl on her back and Little Girl wrapping her little arms around Young Woman's shoulders.

That was just the beginning.

1. String of Pearls (Senecio rowleyanus)
2. Inch plant (Tradescantia zebrina)
3. English Ivy (Hedera Helix)
4. Snake plant (Dracaena trifasciata)
5. Christmas cactus (Schlumbergera bridgesii)
6. Goldilocks (Lysimachia nummularia)
7. Spider plant (Chlorophytum comosum)
8. Aloe Vera (Aloe barbadensis miller)
9. Star Jasmine (Trachelospermum jasminoides)
10. Peace lily (Spathiphyllum)
11. Boston fern (Nephrolepis exaltata)
12. Golden Pothos (Epipremrum aureum)
13. Bird of Paradise (Strelitzia reginae)

...Jesus said,
"Let the children come to me,
and do not hinder them; for to such
belongs the kingdom of heaven."
—Matthew 19:14